I Could Have Been
An Astronaut...
If It Wasn't For
Malachy McAleer

Anthony Bunko

ISBN: 9798655348837

First published 2020 by STRUMMMER PUBLISHING

Email:- anthonybunko@gmail.com

I Could Have Been An Astronaut... If It Wasn't For Malachy McAleer

Hitler was a frustrated geography teacher

Dedicated to: -

All the grownups who have ever had six of the best when

they were in school (adult sex parties don't count)

and lived to tell the tale...

Chapters: -

WHERE ARE THEY NOW - SCHOOL YEAR BOOK

A little bit of the back story...

Ever since he could remember, Jonny Dekka wanted to be an Astronaut: the very first person from Dowlais Flats to walk on the moon.

In his imagination, he pictured his mother showing off to the bingo crowd down the Legion club on the weekend... "Look what my little Dekka's done!" And all the other mothers jealous, cos their own sons would mainly be in prison, be drug dealers, or worse: of all, traffic wardens.

When Dekka was about eight and a bit, he wrote a six-step plan (even way back then, he was quite logical for a working-class kid from a working-class background...).

Step one: go to comprehensive school, stay out of trouble and get good grades.

Step two: go to university, study hard and become the top student. (And try not to get too smelly.)

Step three: be accepted by NASA, in America. Work hard. Be the top student. Try not to get too fat, or shot (or both)!

Step four: become an Astronaut. (For some reason, he wrote the following in brackets after that...(Ground control to Merthyr Tom... take your Prosaic pills and put the kettle on.). He must have seen David Bowie on tele or something, while his mother was spaced out in the kitchen doing the ironing.)

Step five: be the first Welsh person to go in to space, stick a Welsh flag on the moon, and run around like I have just scored the winning goal against St Mary's school in the FA cup final at Wembley.

Step six: come home to a hero's welcome and have a statue in the town - next to that famous boxer, Howard Winalot (but much bigger... and made of gold).

It was a simple plan. Well, things were simple when Dekka was young.

Of course, he hid the plan under the bed from his father; he wouldn't have understood. Fathers never did back in them days.

However, what Dekka didn't count on, was failing so dramatically at the first hurdle.

This is the true...ish story of how a young boy's dream never came true.

This is...

I Could Have Been An Astronaut... If It Wasn't For Malachy McAleer

2 and 2 = clay class blues

Year 1

Sept 1st 1977

Mister Hill's class

9am

PRISON

"And finally, you at the back... wearing that, that... cheap looking blazer..."

Silence

"You. It's *you* I'm talking to, boy."

"Who? Me?"

"Yes, you: you with the black hair. What's your name?"

"Dekka, Sir. Johnny Dekka."

"Dekka. Dekka… Dekkkkkka… That rings a bell. Do you know a 'Royston Dekka,' Dekkkkka?"

The teacher bounds across the room and goes right up to Dekka…

"Well do you, Dekka?"

"No, Sir."

"Shame, lovely lad. One of the best pupils I ever…"

"Sorry, Sir. I misunderstood you. I do know him."

"You do!?"

"Yeah… he's my brother."

"Your brother!?"

"Yes, Sir. This was *his* cheap looking blazer."

"Well, well, well. How's he doing these days?"

"Well, Sir… really well."

"I always knew he'd make something of himself. A fine, fine lad."

"Sorry, Sir, I misunderstood you again: he's not doing well at all."

Silence

"Why?"

"Why, what, Sir?"

"Why isn't he doing well?"

"He's in prison."

"Prison?"

A loud Ooohhhh from the class

"Prison! Royston Dekka is in prison?!"

"Yes, Sir. Three years... Cardiff nick."

A second loud Ooohhhh from the class

"For what?"

"Robbing, Sir."

"Robbing? Are you sure? He didn't seem like the criminal type. He never even had detention."

"Positive. I went to visit him last week. My mother baked him a cake."

"Did it have a file and a false passport in it?"

"That's funny, Maria Jones."

"Thanks, Dekka."

"My Grampa broke out of Colditz after my gran baked him a cake like that."

"Don't talk rubbish, Jenkins."

"I'm not, Sir. I'll bring a photo in tomorrow."

"Of your Grampa, or the cake?"

"Both, Maria Jones. So, there."

Silence

"May I enquire, Dekka, what your brother robbed?"

"The chemist shop, Sir."

"The chemist shop?"

"Yes, Sir. *(quiet)* Drugs."

"Drugs?"

Another loud Ooohhhh from the class

"Yes… and then the Spar shop."

"The Spar shop??"

"Yes, Sir. *(quiet)* Drink… and…"

An extra loud Ooohhhh from the class

Silence

"And what, boy?"

"And what… what, Sir?"

"AND WHAT ELSE DID HE ROB?"

"The butchers."

"Harry, the Butcher?'

"Yes, Sir."

"Why did he rob Harry the Butcher?"

"Sausages."

"Sausages?"

"Ooooooo I luvs sausages I do, Sir."

"Quiet, Carl Cross."

"And me. I love the ones in the tin with beans. Beans means..." *(scratches)* Ohhhh I'm itching.'

"And you, Hannah. And stop scratching, girl."

"I can't help it, Sir. It's my nits."

All the kids move their desks away

"Now, Dekka, why did he pinch sausages?"

"I guess cos he likes sausages, Sir."

"We have sausages on Christmas day. I love Christmas day sausages."

"We don't want to know, Cross."

"Look at the size on this nit. Oh, it's OK... it's only ear wax..."

Hannah tastes it - the kids heave

"Quiet everyone. Dekka, I'm watching you boy. *(loud clap, stands in front of the class...)* Right, class... any questions about your first day at Bishop JR Hartley High School?"

Silence

"Come on, there must be something?"

Silence

"Are we allowed fag breaks, Sir?"

"Who said that?"

"Me Sir: Malachy McAleer. M.A.L.A.C.H.Y."

Mr Hill rushes to back of classroom and stands over the boy

"No, you're not allowed fag breaks, Malachiii. You're only twelve… and put that lighter away."

"Bleedin' hell, Sir… that's not fair."

"Any more language like that my boy, and you'll be up before the headmaster, Mister Gay."

Next desk to them, Dekka bursts out laughing

"What's so funny, Dekka?"

"Nothing, Sir."

"I'm warning you. If you laugh again, you'll be up to see Mister Gay, too."

"Are there two of 'em then, Sir."

"What, Malachiii!?"

"The two Mister Gays, Sir… are they twins?"

"Probably joined at the cane, Malachy."

"Good one, Dekka."

Laughter

"That's it. Malachiii! Dekkkka! Outside!"

"But, Sir..."

"OUT!!!"

The boys go outside and stand in the corridor

Silence

"Hey, Dekka... is your brother really in prison?"

"Nah, I made it up. He's a twat."

"That's hilarious."

"I just hate everyone telling me how good he is.

Laughter

"I like you, Dekka.

"I like you too, Mal...."

A commotion in the corridor stops them in their tracks: they see a wild haired teacher wearing a tabard, dragging a young boy by his hair through the corridor...

"I'll teach you to chew in my class, boy."

"I wasn't, Sir. I wasn't chewing."

"Liar!"

"I'm not, Sir... look... I haven't got any teeth. *(smiles: black teeth)* Too much sherbet when I was a baby."

"Did you spit at me then, boy."

"No, Sir."

"You did, you beast. Finger out."

"No, Sir, please..."

"Do it *(the teacher clamps the boy's finger in a nut cracker. A loud cracking sound rings out in the corridor)* Now, get back to lesson - and if I catch you chewing again, you'll be in real trouble."

The boy limps off in pain, Mental-Evans sees the two boys. He walks up to them, eyeing them up and down.

"First day, is it boys? *(The boys nod)* And in trouble already, is it boys? *(they nod again)* Well, I'll be seeing you around.

Mental-Evans walks down the corridor, singing

"Do I really wanna hurt them... Do I really wanna make 'em cry... Yep."

*As a side note: a young Boy George who was taking a note from his mother to Mister Pope, the sports teacher, excusing him from games, just happened to be walking past at that very moment and thought, 'I'll use 'em lyrics one day'.

Back to the story

"Who the hell was that, Malachy?"

"Mental-Evans... he's the metal work teacher. He scalped a pupil last term with a chisel, just for whistling."

"Bloody hell."

"Anyway, do you always make stuff up then, Dekka?"

"Yeah. Stuff just pops in to my head."

"You make me laugh."

"Thanks. Do you really smoke?"

"Does a bear shit in the woods?"

"Not if it's a polar bear."

"Bloody hell, I never thought of that."

"Anyway, I'm Dekka"

Holds out his hand...

"And I'm Malachy."

"I know: M A L A C H Y."

Antilogarithms are the vile twin of logarithms!

Sept 4th 1977

Dekka's home

6.05pm

MAFIA

Dekka sits in front of the TV trying to tape 'Top of the Pops'. His mother ironing in the corner. Father walks in, no trousers on.

"What's that bloody rubbish on the tele?"

"Ssshh, dad. I'm trying to tape it. It's the Undertones, on Top of the Pops."

"Don't sshh me. Good God, that singer looks like a right spaz."

"Bernard, you can't say that."

"I can, June... it's the seventies. I can say what I like. *(Bernard stands up)* I can say poofters, people of colour, brainstorming, Marathon bars - never Snickers! And don't get me started on starbursts. It's Opel Fruits: OPEL... BLOODY... FRUITS."

"Ohhh, what about the 'S' word Bernard?"

"SEX?"

"I bloody wish... Nooo, mun... SMASH."

"I Luvs Smash, June. Better than real potatoes."

"Will you two be quiet. I'm taping this."

"Then they smash them all to bits*... (Bernard laughs and lies on floor, his feet in air)* Then they smash them all to bits... join in June... *(June joins him)* AND THEY SMASH THEM ALL TO BITS!" AND THEY SMASH THEM ALL TO BITS!" AND THEY SMASH THEM ALL TO BITS!"

"Mam... Dad... shut up. You sound like a more mental Terry and June."

They get back up, June carries on ironing

"I like that presenter, though."

"Which one, June?"

"Him, Bernard... that Jim will fix it bloke. Jimmy Saville. Lovely, lovely bloke. Nice hair."

"Does a lot for charity, I heard. Got his finger in lots of pies."

*I can hear a loud groan from you reading this book. I'm not apologising... in the seventies lots of people did like his hair! *

Back to the front room

"How's school going, love?"

"OK, mam."

"Made any new friends?"

"Yeah."

"Well?"

"Well, what?"

"Well... who have you made friends with??"

"A boy called Malachy McAleer. Now quiet, mam."

"Malachy... Malachy... He sounds like a right dirty, old Pikey. Pikey: another word I can say cos it's the seventies, June."

"He's not a Pikey, dad."

"I bet he lives in a caravan on the Bogie road."

"He doesn't, so there. He lives in the Gurnos... 12A Cherry Grove. It's the one with a fridge in the garden."

"Aye, and I bet he'll get you into trouble. Pikeys always do. Follows them around like a bad smell."

"Mam, tell him."

"Shut up, Bernard. Anyway, did any of the teachers remember your brother?"

Silence

"Well?"

"Well, what?"

"Did any of the teachers remember your brother??"

"One or two. Mam. Quiet, I'm watching this."

"Well, I hope you told them he's a successful IT executive working in Milton Keynes..."

"Who?"

"Your Brother, isn't it."

Silence

"Well, *did* you??

"Did I what??'

Bernard jumps up and hits him with rolled up newspaper

"Did you tell, the fuckin teachers, that your fuckin brother, was a successful IT executive working in fuckin, Milton, fuckin, Keynes? Jesus fuckin wept..."

"Language, Bernard."

"I can fuckin' swear in my own house. I pay my taxes. Not like that Elton John bloke..."

"No, dad. I told them he was in prison."

Bernard laughs

"Johnny, don't say that. You'll be an IT executive working in Milton Keynes one day."

"I don't *want* to be one, mam."

"Too right, son. Come and sit here." *(Bernard taps his lap)*

"No, dad."

"Come on." *(Johnny sighs and sits on his father's lap)* "Look, there's no future in IT. Bloody computers. Tomorrow's bloody chip paper."

"How can a computer be tomorrow's chip paper, Bernard?"

"Don't interrupt me, June. He's going to get a proper job... down the mines."

"No way, dad - I don't like spiders."

"Spiders? Spiders? Never mind the spiders, it's the gas you've got to worry about... Anyway, I guarantee you a job in the pits is a job for life. I say so without a shadow of a doubt that in a hundred - no - *two* hundred years' time, people around here will still be digging coal. Job for life, I'm telling you."

"No, dad. I'm going UP... *(Johnny looks up, his parents follow his stare)* ...instead of down."

"Chimney sweep, is it?"

"Ooohhh just like my Uncle Alan: best chimney sweep in the village. He can get in to any nook or cranny."

"June, your Uncle Alan is a fuckin' midget."

"Alan is *not* a 'fuckin' midget'. He's just small boned."

"Chicken fuckin' boned more like."

"Oh, look at the perfect Mafia family here. Your mother's like Barlon Mando in the Codfather."

"Oh, my mother had it tough."

"What? Her fuckin' bingo pen run out!"

Johnny steps in between them

"But mam, dad... I want to be a..."

All the lights in the house suddenly go off

"Another bloody power cut! Get the candles out of the sideboard, June. Bloody miners...always on bloody strike."

Sept 5th 1977

Schoolyard

12.33pm

DALEKS

Dekka and Malachy stand in the corner of the school yard. Patrolling around the perimeter, is Sister Flip and Sister Flop, the infamous school bullies - sorry, nuns...

"Dekka, look... they haven't got any feet."

"Sshh Malachy, you nutter. They'll hear you."

"They're floating like Daleks. *(Giggles)* We will exterminate... we will exterminate."

The nuns walk near the boys. The boys stand still, afraid to breathe

"Don't forget you two: no swearing, spitting, smoking, running in the corridors, snogging or p...p...petting in the shallow end." *(The two nuns both point at their own groins)*

"Ok, Sister Flop."

"Shall I fist them, Flip?"

"*Frisk* them you mean, Flop."

"I knows what I mean, Flip."

The nuns growl and stroll off. Three boys: Big Murphy and his gang march through the crowd and approach Dekka.

"Oh, first year... giz me your dinner money."

"No. I'm going for cob and chips, now."

"Give it, I said."

"No way."

"Right, Butt... you're having it."

Big Murphy starts to push Dekka...

"Leave me alone, or I'll tell my brother."

"Your brother?"

"Yeah... and he's a right psycho."

"Is he? What's his name then?"

"Royston 'Razorblade' Dekka. He told me if I had trouble, he'll come down and cut you lot up."

Big Murphy stares at him. He calls his gang into a huddle. Heads down they mutter to each other. They break up. Big Murphy faces up to Dekka again.

"*Razorblade Dekka*, you say?"

"Yeah. And he's just got out of prison."

The bullies look at each other again.

"OK, you keep your dinner money, Dekka. And don't forget… if you want anyone beaten up, give us a shout. I'm Big Murphy… and this is my gang."

The other two boys wave in a girly way.

"I'm Dwayne."

"And I'm Martyn with a Y - - not an I."

The gang start to walk away…

"Oh, Big Murphy… can you beat Mister Hill up for us?"

Big Murphy stops dead in his tracks

"WHO… THE… FUCK… are you?"

Big Murphy and his gang spin back around

Silence

"Well!?"

"Malachy McAleer."

"Who?"

"Malachy… M a l a c h y."

The gang start laughing

"What type of name is *that*?"

"It's my type of name. What type of name is *Big Murphy*?"

A loud Ooohhhh from the other schoolkids in the yard

"Never mind my name. For your sake, you better have a brother as well."

"Yeah, I do."

"Is he hard and just got out of prison?"

"Well... he got suspended from nursery last week for head butting some infant kid in the sandpit."

"Well, hard luck Malachy. Dinner money, or else."

"Or else what?"

"Or else I'll punch you."

"Ouch!"

Malachy punches Big Murphy

"You can't punch me, I'm a third year."

"You were going to punch me!"

"*That's* not how it works. Third years beat up the new starters. Ouch! Stop hitting me!"

"Well, give us *your* dinner money."

"That's not the rules."

"I don't care, Big Murphy. Dinner money... or else."

"Or else what?"

"Get ready, Dekka...

Malachy turns to Dekka and then back to Big Murphy

"One... two... three... or this!"

Boosh.

Bam.

Wallop.

All the schoolkids (and a few teachers) in the yard come running to see the scrap.

"FIGHT! FIGHT! FIGHT!"

Nuns carry spud-guns

Sept 5th 1977

Mister Gay's office

2.15pm

HOUDINI

Mr. Gay, the headmaster, stands in his room looking through a pair of binoculars out of the window. There is a knock on the door. One of the teachers pushes Dekka and Malachy into the office...

"Not you two *again*. McAleer and Dekka, isn't it?"

Silence

"Isn't it?"

"Yes, Mister Gay. I'm Johnny Dekka and he's..."

"I know who he is. Now, why are you here this time?"

Silence

"WHY, I said?"

"Fighting, Mister Gay."

"FIGHTING!?"

"In the yard."

"In the Yard. *Tut...tut... tut...* Now, how many days have you been at this school?"

Silence

"Well?"

"Are you talking to us?"

"Of *course,* I'm talking to you, McAleer. Is there anyone else in the room? Well, is there?"

"There could be someone in that cupboard?"

"What?"

"Hiding in the cupboard... over there. Probably Mister Pope, the sports teacher."

"*Why* would Mister Pope be hiding in my cupboard?"

"Maybe he likes cupboards."

"Are you thick, McAleer?"

"He could be one of those 'gimps', Sir?"

"Gimp? Gimp? What do you know about *gimps*, Dekka?"

Silence.

"Well?"

"I didn't mean a *gimp*."

"What did you mean, then?"

"Who?"

"You, Dekka, you!"

"Is a gimp some kind of pervy PE teacher then, Mister GAYYYY?"

"Shut it, McAleer."

"Sorry, I meant a gerbil."

"A gerbil?? That's nothing like a gimp, Dekka."

"Is a gimp like a rat thing then, Sir? Cos if it is, my grans got a massive black gimp living in her coal cwtch?"

"No, McAleer, it's not."

"Come to think of it, I *did* mean a gimp, Sir."

"Is there something wrong with you, Dekka?"

"I don't think so. Do I look ill?"

"Dekka, you are testing my patience and you don't want to test my patience, do you, boy?"

"No, Mister Gay."

"That's right. Now, I don't want to hear you mention anything about *gimps* or Mister Pope hiding in the cupboard, ever again. Understand?"

"OK, I promise not to tell anyone about Mister Pope being a gimp and hiding in your cupboard?"

"He's not *in* the damn cupboard."

Mister Gay marches over to the cupboard and swings open the door…

"See. It's empty."

He slams the cupboard door shut.

"Maybe there's a secret panel at the back…"

"What, McAleer?"

"Like Houdini, Sir."

"I'll Houdini you in a minute. Right, you two: how many days have you been in this school?"

"Umm, three."

"It's Friday, McAleer. You've been here five days."

"I thought it was Wednesday, sir?"

"Why would you think it's Wednesday?"

"I lose track of days. Are you sure?"

"Yes, I'm sure, McAleer. I'm the Headmaster… it's Friday… we just had fish."

"The seed of the devil."

"*What*, Dekka?"

"That's what my father says. Fish: the seed of the devil - especially peppered mackerel."

"Shut up. You have been in this school for five days, and in those five days, how many times have you been sent to see me?"

Silence.

"WELL??"

"You told us to shut up, Mister Gay."

"JUST ANSWER ME, McAleer. How many times in those five days have you been sent to my office?!"

"Three times, sir."

"No, it's FIVE. FIVE times in your first FIVE days."

"Sorry, Mister Gay. I thought it was Wednesday again..."

"Arrgghh! Right, McAleer, hold out your hands."

"But, Sir... I'm just not good at telling days..."

"Maybe he's 'Days-lexic', Mister Gay?"

"Shut it, Dekka. McAleer, hands out."

"But..."

WHACK

WHACK

"Now, how's that, boy?"

"Not as hard as when my stepfather hits me with his belt."

"Oh, we'll see about that."

WHACK

WHACK

WHACK

WHACK

"Stand over there. Now you, Dekka."

"But, Mister Gay?"

"Hands out."

"*I know* it's Friday, Sir. We're having fish fingers for tea - and my father doesn't hit me with a belt."

"Hands out!"

"He doesn't even wear a belt."

"Hands out!"

"He hardly even wears trousers."

"NOW."

WHACK

WHACK

WHACK

WHACK

WHACK

WHACK

"How was that? Harder than your father-in-law hits you?"

"Father- in-law, Sir? I'm only twelve... this isn't Ebbw Vale."

"*Stepfather,* I meant."

'I haven't got a stepfather... and my father don't hit me."

"Well, maybe he should. Now, get out of my sight."

"Us?"

"YES. YOU. OUT!"

The boys leave the room.

"Do you think he really is glad to be g...a...y?"

"Shut up, Malachy."

Ox-bow lakes are small ponds in disguise

Sept 8th 1977

Mister Hill's class

9.01pm

TEST

Mister Hill stands at the front of the class, checking his pocket watch...

"Right, books away. English literature test, two hours. No talking, no copying. *(Big moan from the kids)* Ready... *(he looks at his watch again)* four, three, two, one..."

Hannah rushes in, in her pyjamas, goggles and arm bands, holding a brick...

"Sorry I'm late. I was looking for a brick."

"What are you dressed like that for, Hannah?"

"Diving test, Sir."

"It's an English lit test, Hannah."

"Maria Jones said we were doing a diving test."

Everyone looks at Maria Jones

"Did I? I must have made a mistake, sorry Sir.' *(Maria smirks)*

"Just sit-down Hannah*. (Mister Hill looks at his watch)* Right... start."

Silence

Clock ticking

Five minutes go by...

"Sir?"

"*What*, Malachiii?"

"I haven't got a pen."

"You haven't got a pen?"

"I just said that."

"*Why* haven't you got a pen?"

"I didn't realise I needed one, sir."

"You're sitting an exam, boy. What did you think you would need?"

"Hiking boots... a compass... a map?"

"Don't be stupid boy... borrow mine."

He pulls a rather odd-looking pen out of his pocket and hands it to the boy

9.15am

Silence

"Sir... sir."

"What Jenny?"

Jenny heaves

"Hannah's picking her scabs and eating them, sir."

"Hannah!"

"I didn't have any breakfast, Sir..."

"Let's have one! *(Crossy walks across and eats one)* Mmm... like soggy crisps."

"Sit back down Cross - and Hannah, eat your scabs at breaktime. Now, quiet."

10.00am

Silence

"Frankie Pratt... are you asleep?"

Frankie's head is down on his desk

"I'm... thinking, Sir."

"Of Jenny Cabbage's jugs."

"Malachiii!!! I'm warning you. Frankie, think with your eyes *open*."

"Mmmm Jenny... Mmmm Jugs. Mmmm penis..."

"Frankie... behave."

Silence

Clock ticking away

Malachy's hand goes up

"What *now*, Malachiii???"

"I've finished, Sir."

"Finished!?"

Everyone looks at him...

"Yep. Do you want your pen back, Sir?"

"You can't have finished, boy. Christine Lee's only on question three, and she's ten times brainier than you; she's from the posh part of town."

Mr Hill picks up Malachy's paper

"You haven't written anything for questions two... nor three... five, six... eight... nine nor eleven..."

"My mind's gone blank, Sir."

"Hang on... what the hell have you written for question four? What do you mean, 'Corn Flakes'?"

"That's the answer, Sir: Corn Flakes."

Mr Hill points across the room at Carl Cross

"Carl Cross, *don't* write Corn Flakes down."

"Why not, Sir?"

"Because the question asks you to explain, in no more than six hundred words, 'what was the moral and social message behind Shakespeare's play the 'Merchant of Venice'."

"The Merchant of Venus?"

"No, Maria Jones: Venice. *Venice*."

"Mmmm Merchant... Mmmm Venus. Mmmm... penis."

"Quiet, Frankie! Class, we've been studying him all term..."

"I study mine Venus five times a day... Mmmm."

"Uch a fi, Frankie."

"You luvs it, Maria Jones."

"Sir, sir, can I go to the toilet?"

"No, Jenny, you can't... The Merchant of Venice... Macbeth, Romeo and Juliet..."

"... Batman and Robin."

"Shut up, Dekka."

Crossy climbs up on his desk

'Dara... dara... dara... dara... Batman!"

Mister Hill doesn't notice… he's lost in his own world…

"Juliet… O Romeo, Romeo! Wherefore art thou, Romeo? Deny thy father and refuse thy name; or, if thou wilt not… be but sworn of my love."

"Me, Sir, me… me."

"OK, Carl Cross. Continue."

Carl still standing on desk

"And I'll no longer be a *(pause)* cat… a… pult."

"Is that Welsh, Sir?

"It's English, Hannah, English. You moron. The greatest English ever written."

"Sir, I *really* need the toilet."

"No, Jenny. And get down, Carl Cross!"

"Is it something to do with ox-tail soup lakes then, Sir?"

"What, Carl??"

"Ox-tail soup lakes… there's always a question about them."

"That's geography - and its 'Ox-bow lakes'!"

"What flavour are Ox-bow lakes, Sir?"

"I bet it's one of 'em posh soups you get in the Co-op."

"I luvs 'em, Marie Jones."

"And me, Crossy."

Hannah starts to move across the floor on her bum like a dog

"Hannah, *what* are you doing now?"

"I think I caught ring worms from my dog, Sir."

"Mmmm things... Mmmm rings... Mmmm... penis."

"Shut up, Frankie."

"But, Sir... Dekka told me there were ox-tail soup lakes in Scot-er-land."

"Are you an actual moron, Cross?"

"No, Sir... I'm an actual Catholic."

All the class make the sign of the cross and in unison...

"In the name of the Father, and the Son, and cheese on toast."

"Mmmm father... Mmmm son... Mmmm penis."

"Frankie, be quiet! Now, will everyone carry on with the test..."

"I need the toilet."

"No, Jenny."

"So, to be clear, Sir, there's no tomato soup lakes either?"

"No, Cross, and there are no such thing as 'soup lakes' ... and Jonny Dekka. Keep your imagination to yourself."

"Sir, who *is* this 'Snakespeare' bloke?"

"To pee, or not to pee!"

"I'm going to pee myself now, in a minute."

"It's Shakespeare, Hannah. Not 'Snakespeare'. And Jenny, put your jumper back on."

"But, I'm hot."

"Mmmm... hot tottie."

"Cover up, girl!"

"But I'm going to be a model, sir."

"For who? The Seven Dwarves?"

"Tell Malachy, sir."

"Jumper on, Jenny... Hannah, why have you written 'beans on toast' for question four?"

"I...I...I *(Hannah starts to cry)* I don't know... I don't like corn flakes....and that's what I like for breakfast."

"For f... f...u...c never mind. Write what you like... You're going to end up in the clay class, anyway."

Bell rings.

"Put your papers on my desk... and don't run."

They all run out of class

"Walk. I said WALK."

When they leave, Mr Hill looks at the papers and throws them in the bin, then he slumps down in his chair.

"Why didn't I just join the bloody army?"

Mister Foley was 2 foot 3 inches in his bare feet

Feb 9th 1976

Corridor

10.24am

STRIKE

"MCALEER! MCALEER! STOP running in the corridor!"

"I wasn't running, Mister Gaaaaaay."

"You were, boy. I saw you. I saw you with my very own eyes."

"I'm sure I wasn't, Mister Gaaaaay. Maybe everyone else was just going slow."

"What?"

"Going slow."

"What are you on about now, boy?"

"Everyone else, Mister Gaaaaay… maybe they were just going slow."

"Slow?!"

"Like in slow motion… or like them people on strike."

"Strike! Who's on strike?"

"The bin men are always on strike. There's bags of rubbish in my street reaching up to my bedroom window, and you should see the size of the rats… massive they is."

"What is that to do with you running in the corridor, boy?"

"They go slow as well, Mister Gaaaaay."

"Who? The rats?"

"No, the bin men, Mister Gaaaay. Didn't you listen to a word I just said?"

"Don't talk to me like that, McAleer."

"But I was just saying…"

"I don't care. Just shut up I said, and come here boy when I'm speaking to you."

"But, Mister Gaaaaay, I've got to go."

"Here, I said. Now."

Footsteps…

"Oh, I can see you've been fighting again, McAleer. Will you *ever* learn, boy?"

"I haven't been fighting, Mister Gaaaay."

"Stop lying, boy! You have a black eye and a cut on your lip. You must have been fighting, so don't lie to me again."

"I wasn't lying... I wasn't fighting. Honest."

"Well, if you weren't fighting, boy... how did you end up in such a state? Did you walk into a door?"

Silence

"*Well*, McAleer?"

"Hum, err... my... my... OK, I was fighting, Mister Gaaaaay."

"Thought so. Get to my office, now. Maybe six of the best will help take that fighting and lying streak out of you - and DON'T RUN!!!"

School dinners are made from leftover dog food

Oct 17th 1977

Mister Hill's class

3pm

ASTRONAUT

"Christine Lee... what do you want to do when you leave school?"

"She's going to be a ginger vampire, Sir. She will drink your blood... aaaaarrrgh."

"Malachiii... quiet."

"University to become a teacher, just like you, Mister Hill."

"You specky eyed bitch - sorry - *witch*."

"Malachiii, keep your comments to yourself. Good, Christine. Hannah?"

"I'm umm... I'm gonna work in... umm... Wimpy's, Sir. Making burgers... and maybe umm fries - oh, and milkshakes. Banana ones. I love bananas."

Crossy gets up on table and makes monkey noises

"Cross... what are you doing?"

"I'm a monkey, Sir. Eating bananas."

More monkey noises...

"Just get down, boy."

"But, Sir..."

"Down! And you, Dekka?"

"What?"

"What do you want to do? Hopefully, you *won't* go to prison like your brother."

"Astronaut, Sir."

A loud Ooohhhh from the rest of the class

"What?"

"An astro...nut, he said, Sir."

"Quiet, Cross."

"Like Neil Armstrong... walking on the moon and stuff."

"Be serious, boy."

"I am, Sir."

"I'm sorry to disappoint you, but Astronauts don't come from Dowlais flats."

"Is that because of the drying rooms?"

"*What*, Malachiii?"

"Because someone would nick their spacesuits if they hung them up in the drying rooms to dry in the flats, Sir. I know I would."

"My nan would pinch his helmet for her fish."

"*What*, Maria Jones??"

"My gran's fish tank blew up last week and killed all her fish, so she would probably use Dekka's space helmet to keep her new fish in."

Silence

"Sir?"

"What now, Hannah?"

"So... is the reason Dekka can't be an Astronaut, cos of the drying rooms and Maria's gran's fish tank?"

"No, Hannah. Only proper people like Americans and Russians become Astronauts and go to space..."

"Don't they have Dowlais flats in them countries, Sir?"

"No, Maria Jones. Right, Dekka... I'll just put you down that you will work down the mines..."

"I'm not working down the mines."

"It's a job for life, boy. It's a job for life... it's a job for life."

"What about that chimp, Sir?"

Monkey noises

"Cross! Get off the bloody table. Now, what are you talking about, Malachiii?"

"That chimp that drove to the moon in a rocket... and messed about."

"My uncle had a chimp once... Boz, his name was. Big black thing."

"Did it look like Doris the dinner lady, Jenkins?"

"The monkey was less hairy than Doris, Maria Jones."

Laughter

"Did *he* go to the moon?"

"No, Crossy, but he could lick his own goolies."

"I heard Doris can do that too."

"Maria Jones... you're on fire."

"Cheers, Dekka."

Laughter

"CLASS, STOP THIS AT ONCE! Jenkins, go and see Mister Gay and tell him what you just said."

"What did I say, Sir?"

"You said your Uncle's chimp Boz can lick his own goolies!"

Giggles can be heard through the class

"Malachiii, get out!"

"But I was only saying what he said..."

"I don't care... get out! NOW!"

"Arrrgghhhhhh."

Jenkins and Malachy walk out...

Silence

"Mmmm... I can lick my own goolies mmmm."

"WHO SAID THAT? WHO SAID THAT?"

Silence

"DEKKA!?"

"What, Sir?"

"Was that you??"

"Well, I've never tried, Sir. I will have a go tonight and let you know in the morning."

"It was Frankie who said he can lick his own goolies like Jenkin's Uncle's monkey did, Sir..."

"Get out, Maria Jones."

"But, Sir, I was only saying what Frankie said."

"OUT!"

Marie Jones walks out

"What are 'goolies', Sir? "

"Hannah, get out - and you, Frankie."

"For what??"

"You're twelve years old, boy... why are you talking about licking your... goo... goo... Just get OUT!"

They stare at each other

Silence

"Shall I show you, Sir?"

"OUT!!!"

Frankie and Hannah walk out

Silence

Mister Hill taking deep breaths...

"Sir..."

"What *now*, Dekka?"

"*I am* going to be an Astronaut."

"OK, OK Dekka *(scribbling on paper)* See... it's down in print, now. Let's see how far that gets you."

"Sir..."

"What, Cross?"

"Well, if Dekka's going to be an Astro...nut, I want to change mine job from working on the production line in Hoovers, to being a cowboy."

"A cowboy!?"

"Fighting Indians, and I want Champion the Wonder horse... and a big black hat and a gold tooth..."

"Cross, you are mental. Now get out."

"But..."

"OUT!"

Crossy walks out

"Well, if Carl Cross is now a cowboy, I wanna be a 16th century chambermaid... look at these!"

Jenny points her chest out

"Jenny, stop sticking your ta...ta...tatties out and get out of my class."

Jenny walks out

"Sir... Sir..."

"I don't WANT to know, Dekka. OUT!"

"But, Sir..."

"GET OUT! And you Maria, and you Reece, and you Christine..."

"Why, Mister Hill, I haven't said anything?"

"Cause you're a ginger vampire - OUT! In fact, ALL of you get out. NOOOW!!!"

Mr Hill looks at an empty chair

"And you can fuck off as well... aaarrgghhhh!!!"

They all walk out, leaving Mister Hill by his desk. He twitches. He takes his tie off and puts it on his head and starts mumbling to himself.

Mister Gay's voice comes over the tannoy...

"Sister Flip, Sister Flop... we have a 'situation' in room 1C. Teacher down... teacher down... sort it."

The two nun's ears prick up

"Get the gun and the strait-jacket out of the cupboard, Flip."

"Ooohhhh great, Flop. Can I fist him?"

"Probably, Flip, probably."

Oct 17th 1975

Boys' Toilets

3.45pm

GOOLIES

"Dekka, that was genius... pure genius. You really had Mister Hill going then. He went nuts... an Astronaut. Brilliant."

"But I do want to be an Astronaut, Malachy."

Laughter

"Yeah, OK."

"I do. I've always dreamt of going up into space..."

"Shut up!"

"Honest. Ever since I was a little kid. Can you imagine it*... (pause)* finding out what's up there?"

"There's nothing up there, idiot. Just space and the moon, and some monkey licking his own goolies, apparently."

"I can do that!"

"Frankie... are you in the cubicle?"

"Mmmm... do you want me to show you how to do it? Mmmm bend Mmmm tongue... Mmmm penis."

"No thanks, Frankie."

Laughter

Silence

"So, what about you then Malachy... what do you want to be?"

"Me? Nothing."

"There must be *something* you want to be? Footballer or a Comedian... probably a boxer: 'One-Punch McAleer'!"

Silence

"Come on, you can tell me."

"There's nothing."

"There *must* be!"

"OK, OK, Dekka, if you must know... the only thing I want is to get bigger and stronger."

"So, you do wanna be a boxer... then you can beat Big Murphy up again."

"No - so I can stop my stepdad from beating my mother and me up every night. Is that OK with you?"

"Ooohhh. I'm... sorry."

"Are you? It's not as good as flying off in to space or being a cowboy, or a maths teacher... but it's important to me and my mother."

Silence

Bell rings

Pen-y-dre spelt backwards is evil

Oct 18th 1977

Mister Hill's Ex-Class

9.00am

CHICKEN

Lots of noise from the class. Most of the kids messing about. Door opens. Smart woman walks in...

"Good morning... One C."

Still lots of noise

"Good morning... One C."

Still noise...

"GOOD MORNING, ONE C..."

Silence

"Who're you?"

"I'm Miss Chicken, your new teacher. And you are?"

"Malachy McAleer."

"Who?"

"Malachy... M A L A C H Y."

"Wow, that's a wonderful, poetic sounding name. Is it Irish by any chance?"

"Is what Irish?"

"Your name. Is it Irish?"

"No, it's Malachy McAleer. I just told you. Are you deaf or what?"

Crossy gets to his feet, he thinks she's deaf. He speaks loudly and does sign language...

"My name is Carl Cross, Miss. I'm from Galon Uchaf."

"I'm not deaf, Carl, now sit down."

"Mmmm... fresh... Mmmm... fish... Mmmm... penis."

"You must be Frankie Pratt."

"Mmmm... yeah... Mmmm... Miss... Mmmm... penis."

"Hello, Miss. I'm Maria Jones. Where's Mister Hill?"

"He's not well."

"Will he be in tomorrow?"

"You will probably not be seeing Mister Hill for a while..."

"HURRAY!"

Crossy gets on desk and makes monkey noises

"Will you get down, please?"

"That's Carl Cross, Miss. He always climbs on the desk when he's excited."

"Why?"

"Cos... he's excited, Miss. Dekka just told you that. Dull as well as deaf..."

"Quiet, Malachy."

Door opens. Mister Pope, the pervy sports teacher in his tight red shorts, walks in and puts his foot on a chair...

"Hey, Chick, I'm the 'Pope-monster'. I can do sixty-eight press-ups, thirty-four burpees and..." *(cocky smile)*

"And..?"

"And if you're wondering, that ain't a shuttlecock in my shorts... it's alllllll me. And if you want anyone of these wasters beaten up, just call me Chick... *(stands by the door)* 7...3...4...5...5...8."

The 'pope monster' leaves

"Miss..."

"What now, Malachy?"

"It *is* a shuttlecock, Miss. I've seen him in the showers... willy like a jelly bean."

"I luvs jelly beans me, especially the jelly ones."

"You must be Hannah..."

"How did you know that Miss? Are you psychic?"

"Cos she's heard how dull you are, ain't it, Miss."

"Quiet, Malachy. Now, Carl Cross, get down off that desk or I will get you down."

"Shoot him down, Miss."

"Malachy... don't talk rubbish."

"Not with a proper gun, Miss... with a stun gun... like in 'Star Trek'."

"I haven't got a stun gun."

"You can borrow mine if you want, Miss!"

"Who are you?"

"I'm Jenkins, Miss. Colin Jenkins."

"Well, I hope you haven't got a stun gun in your satchel, Colin."

Miss Chicken laughs.

"Of course not, Miss. It's in my shed, with my other guns."

"Other guns!?"

"Yeah, I have loads. I have a couple of AK47's... two rifles, three shotguns and a tank."

"A tank!?"

"Don't listen to him, Miss, he's lying."

"I'm not lying, Dekka. I have got a tank."

"Yeah - a hot water tank. Anyway, Miss, just pull Crossy down by his ears."

"I can't do that, Dekka."

"Pull him off by his tail then, Miss."

"He hasn't got a tail, Maria Jones."

"All monkeys have tails, Miss."

"He's not a bleeding monkey. Jesus Christ, no wonder Mister Hill had a nervous breakdown."

A massive loud Ooohhhh from the class

Crossy sits down

"Is he in the nuthouse then, Miss?"

"No, he's not, Malachy. Right, let's get your books out and get some work done."

Silence

"Miss? Miss Chicken?"

"Yes, Malachy?"

"Have you ever... ever... ever... laid an egg?"

Giggles

"Not Funny, Malachy."

"That was, Miss."

"It wasn't. Dekka."

"If you do, Miss, can I have it?"

"*What*, Carl Cross?"

"If you lay an egg, Miss... can I have it? Cos we can't afford real eggs, see."

"Miss?"

"What, Dekka?"

"If Crossy can't afford real eggs, what eggs *can* he afford?"

"I'm not interested in Carl's eggs."

"We have jokin' ones."

"What, Carl?"

"My mother gives us jokin' eggs, Miss."

>   *Silence as they all sit there thinking...*

"Miss. Miss. Miss..."

"Maria Jones... I don't know what joking eggs are."

"No, Miss, I think there's something wrong with Hannah..."

>   *Hannah is itching between her legs. Miss Chicken walks up to her...*

"What's wrong, Hannah?

"I think I've got thrust, Miss."

All the others move way from Hannah except Frankie, who watches her intently.

"Mmmm... Girl... Mmmm... troubles... Mmmm... penis."

Silence

"Why don't you ask Crossy what a jokin' egg is, Miss?"

"OK, I will Jenny. Carl?

"What, Miss?"

"What is a jokin' egg?"

Rest of the class move in, one of them falls off the table

Silence

Silence

"It's not a real egg, Miss."

"We know that, but what the fuckin' hell is it?"

"Stop swearing, Malachy."

"But I wanna know what a bloody jokin' bloody egg is!"

Suddenly, the door opens: Mister Gay and Sisters Flip and Flop enter. The two nuns are crying...

"Sooooo... *this* is the class that sent Mister Hill to the nuthouse."

Everyone stares at their desks

"Now, One C… I have some terrible, terrible news…"

"Sister Flop is pregnant?"

"And Sister Flip is the father?"

"Dekka and Maria Jones, come to my office later and I'll show you who is pregnant."

All the kids are dying to laugh… Christine Lee smiles

"Are you smiling, girl?"

"No, Mister Gay."

"I think you is. Mister Mental-Evans, sort that reprobate out this instant."

Mister Evans appears dressed like Leatherface from 'Texas Chainsaw Massacre'. He drags Christine out by her hair.

"Right… I'm sorry to say that today at 8am, the Pope died."

Silence

Everyone stares down at their desks

The nuns sob loudly. Carl Cross looks about, confused. He jumps to his feet…

"Yippee. Mister Pope is dead, Mister Pope is dead."

He runs about the room

"It's not 'Mister Pope', Cross. He's not dead. He's out there... adjusting his shuttlecock. The 'Pope' is dead, Cross... the *Pope*."

Silence

"Is that his brother, then?"

"Just like the rest of your family, Cross... not all there. The *Pope* is the head of the Catholic Church."

"So... he's just a *head*?"

"What?"

"Like in a big jar, on the altar?"

"*What*, Cross??"

"Like a pickled onion, cos I luvs pickled onions me... but they give me terrible wind."

"Real pickled onions or jokin' ones, Cross?"

"Dekka, don't you get involved. Cross, I'll pickle you in a minute, now. Everyone get down on your knees and say a prayer."

"All of us?"

"Yes, McAleer... all of you... on your knees. (**Points at Miss Chicken**) And you woman. Hurry, hurry."

"Pray for what, Mister Gay?"

"For the *Pope*, Cross."

"Mister Pope?"

"Cross, say Mister Pope one more time and Sister Flop will make you squeal like a pig. *(Sister Flop makes an evil face)* Now, on your knees, face the front, close your eyes… and say a silent prayer."

Silence

Everyone with eyes looking down

SILENT PRAYER

"What you doing, McAleer?"

Malachy is facing sideward

"I'm facing Dekka, Mister Gaaaaay."

"This is not a laughing matter, McAleer… turn *this* way."

Silence

Malachy looks about…

"Our father that FARTS in Cefn…"   *(fart sound)*

"Who did that? Who did it??"

Silence

"Right. Sister Flip, Sister Flop… sniff test."

The nuns start to sniff the kids' bums and Miss Chickens. They get closer to Malachy. He panics…

"Ohhh, that's disgusting Dekka. Haven't pooped yourself, have you?"

"Mental-Evans, take Dekka down to the dungeon and strip him naked."

"But it wasn't me, Sir!"

"He smells like gone off eggs, Sir..."

"Real ones or jokin' ones, Malachy?"

"Jokin' ones, Crossy."

"How could you, boy? Break wind on the same day as the Pope died."

"It wasn't me, Mister Gay."

"Yes, Mister Pope is dead. YEESSSSSSS."

"Mental-Evans, take this Carl Cross down as well."

Black Jacks turn kid's teeth green

Dekka couldn't believe the trouble he's got into mainly because of his Pikey – sorry - his best mate, Malachy...

MALACHY.

He vowed it would be different after the Christmas school holiday:

"No more getting into trouble. *I'm* going to be top pupil. Think 'good', think... *Astronaut*."

NEW TERM

Jan 5th 1978

Assembly

6pm

BRAT

Mr Gay stands on the main assembly stage after school, talking to two school inspectors who are sitting on two small chairs in the hall...

"Education to the power of one. No: education plus two Education... no. Education... education... education... result, results... results...government led initiatives developing the next generation... nourishing them, watching them turn in to young adults... Teachers, setting the tone, building a warm environment, mentoring, nurturing. The modern teacher is the pupil's third parent... a positive role model. Education, education, education."

The two inspectors nod politely and write notes down on their pads. Mister Gay bangs the table.

"BOLLOCKS, BOLLOCKS and BIGGER BOLLOCKS. Kids! I hate every single one of the snotty little wasters. Spotty, horny little upstarts in cheap Lipton blazers. The parents are no better... smoking like chimneys, drinking like fishes... the bingo crowd, voting Labour like sheep. Neutered at birth, they should be drowned like kittens."

He paces around the stage.

"I had a dream last night, no - a bloody nightmare: we lived in a world where teachers weren't allowed to smack children. Imagine that... Jesus wept. It would be anarchy. *Hundreds* of little Johnny Rottens running amok, smoking dope, swearing, spitting and upsetting our queen."

Pause. He takes a deep breath.

"NO. No, No - over my dead body. Kids come to school to be hit. In America, they go to school to get shot at. They expect it... they enjoy it... tests have been carried out. Allegedly, eight out of ten cats - sorry, *kids* - only learn properly if the information is beaten into them."

He smiles at the school inspectors.

"What's a black eye, or a few broken ribs compared to a half decent education, I say."

The both inspectors' jot down more observations in their note pads.

"Tut, tut, tutty tut.   That's why I run special teacher training sessions to ensure my staff are in the right frame of mind, got the right tools and techniques to run a successful term."

The stage lights dim

"So, contestants - sorry, *teachers* - come on down and 'beat on the brats'."

The Ramones song, 'beat on the brat' pumps out of the sound system. Three teachers and two nuns race on to the stage like they are appearing on some manic game show. They all sit down facing the inspectors except Sister Flip who still bounces around. Calmly, Mental-Evans walks over to her and tasers her. When she comes too, she sits down as well.

"Ladies and Gentlemen of the Educational Board, we have a newcomer today, a Miss Chicken. Welcome."

"Thank you, Mister Gay."

"Don't interrupt me, Miss Chicken…. anyway, she will be competing against our reigning champion… Mister Mental-Evans. Mister Pope, too, and of course… Sister Flip and Sister Flop."

Sister Flop shoots peas out of her pea shooter. One of them hits one of the inspectors on the neck…

"So, let's bring out our first, victim… sorry, sorry, sorry… Fraudante slip - pupil, I mean, on. Mister Mental-Evans can you do the honours."

Mister Mental-Evans disappears off stage and then reappears dragging a boy onto the stage and pushes him onto the floor, the boy appears petrified

"Right, Miss Chicken, you get to answer the questions first. *(Nuns growl at her)* This boy, this animal more like… didn't hand his homework in on time. His excuse was… *(changes his voice)* 'My father had a heart attack and we went to the hospital.'

Mister Gay holds up the letter. The other teachers shake their heads.

"The question is, Miss Chicken, what is the punishment?"

"Castrate the little twat."

"Settle down, Mister Pope, settle down."

"Miss Chicken?"

"Well, Mister Gay... I'd make sure the boy was OK, and I'd ask him to do it when his father is better."

"You can't be fuckin' serious. What planet is she on? Planet soft-arse??"

"Miss Chicken, I agree with Sister Flop... this boy's father is not only a complete loser, but he's also a fully signed up member of the Protestant Party. There's no excuse for late homework."

"But..."

"No excuse, Miss Chicken. Mister Pope... *(thumb down)* ... the floor is yours."

Mister Pope runs over, sits on the boy's chest. He pulls marker pen out of his shorts and writes something on the boy's forehead. The teacher sits back down. Mister Gay pulls boy off the floor and checks his head.

"Excellent, Mister Pope... but how many times I have got to tell you there's only one W in twat'?"

The boy starts to slowly walk off the stage

"Now, this completely separate boy *(Mister Gay pulls back the same boy)* was caught running like a lunatic in the corridor..."

Mister Mental-Evans throws him to floor again.

"I wasn't running. I have a built-up shoe."

"Like this boy, I stand corrected. Shut it, Jones. Well, Miss Chicken... punishment?"

"I'd pull him to one side, and explain the dangers of running in the corridor to him and others."

The other teachers all turn slowly towards her...

"Look at Florence fucking Nightingale... Jesus H Christ. She'll be tucking him up in bed next, and giving him a bowl of soup... and an Arthur hank."

"I must agree with Sister Flip, Miss Chicken. These creatures don't learn unless they feel the pain. Mister Evans... open the case."

Mister Mental-Evans smirks and picks out some instruments from his black briefcase, the boy starts crying and tries to crawl away.

"Morgan, stop that sobbing, boy, or Mister Evans will give you something to sob about."

Mister Mental-Evan pulls the boy back to the centre of the stage. He takes a pliers and snaps the boy's fingernail off and holds it up in air. Sister Flop opens her mouth. He pops the nail in the nun's gob. The two school inspectors nod their heads in approval...

"Count yourself lucky, Edwards, Mister Evans is in such a lenient mood. Miss Chicken, if you get the last question wrong, I'd ask yourself if you are cut out for the rigors of comprehensive school education... or you might consider doing what woman do best: ironing, cooking or the cleaning of the household."

Mister Gay does the actions of sweeping

"Right, this brand-new yob *(He grabs the same poor boy again)* was caught red-handed, bunking lessons."

"Fucking hell..."

"And swearing... what is the punishment, Miss chicken?"

"Well, I'd *(she looks at the others, they mock her)* .... I'd take him to the science lab *(they all close in)*... and then I'd burn his nuts with a Bunsen burner."

All the others clap and cheer

"First class, Miss Chicken! We'll make a teacher out of you yet. Brothers and Sisters, let's end this session on a positive note... let's 'beat on the brrrraaaaatttttt'"

They start beating him up. The school inspectors start clapping and then race on to the stage and start booting the boy as well.

Jan 26th 1978

Behind the school hall

1.30pm

SMOKIN'

Behind the Sports Hall: Dekker, Jenkins, Frankie stand about shivering in their PE kits. Malachy appears in a parka jacket…

"Hey, it's the ant-hill mob."

"Funny, Malachy, just cos you bunked games."

"I wasn't built for Cross country runs, Dekka."

The others are all shivering, watching Malachy smoking

"I'm bloody freezing."

"Have a drag then, Dekka. It'll warm you up."

"No, I hate smoking."

"Pass it here, Mal..."

Jenkins takes a drag

"Oooooo lovely, I've been smoking since I was six. Woodbine and all..."

"You haven't, Jenkins."

"I have, too, Dekka."

"Women love smokers. Turns them wild and mmmmm wet."

"How do you know, Frankie?"

"Magazines... mmmmmmmm."

"What? Big breasted women humps twelve year old smokers magazine?"

"Mmmm... humps... Mmmm... lumps... Mmmm... penis."

"Dekka, everyone smokes..."

"No they don't Malachy."

"Starsky and Hutch both smoke."

"They're actors, Jenkins. They're not real fags."

"What fags are they then, Dekka? Joking ones, like Crossy's eggs?"

"Piss off, Jenkins."

"Don't take it out on me cos you're too chicken to have a fag like real men."

"Jenkins, you're *twelve*."

"Is it cos astronauts ain't allowed to smoke?"

"No, Malachy, don't be stupid."

"Have a drag then, go on."

"No."

"Yellow-bellied chicken Astronaut!"

"Ok, pass it here... one drag. Happy now?'*(coughs)*

Voice bellows out from somewhere...

"DEKKA! STOP RIGHT WHERE YOU ARE, BOY."

"Oh, shit... it's Mental-Evans..."

Mr Mental-Evans appears next to them with a crazed look in his eye

"Dekka... Malachy... come with me."

"But, Sir..."

"Don't but me, Dekka, boy. The rest of you, out of my sight. Walk, Dekka, walk... and you, Malachy... while you still can!"

He cracks his knuckles with glee

Headmonsters, headmonsters, headmonsters

Jan 26th 1978

Mister Gay's office

1.48pm

QUIRK

Mister Mental-Evans leads Malachy and Dekka in to Mister Gay's office. Mister Gay is dressed in a bath robe and slippers and he is practising his golf swing with the cane...

"Stone the crows, not you two again? Tut, tut, and titty tutty rolly poley. What is it *this* time?"

"This one's been... smoking, Mister Gay."

"Smoking..."

"Like a chimney."

"And Malachy's been bunking."

"Bunking..."

"Yeah, like aa... aaa... big bunk...er."

"I haven't got time for this. Mister Mental-Evans, go to town on them."

"Really? *(Mister Gay nods his head.... Evans is over the moon)* Thank you, thank you! This is like Halloween... my favourite funerals... and films about Nazis all rolled into one. I won't let you down, Mister Gay."

Mr Mental-Evans starts to unroll plastic sheets and sharpen his knives. The boys look nervous...

"But I don't smoke, Sir. He made me do it... I only wanted to keep warm."

He points at Malachy...

"We'll see about that, Dekka."

"What does that mean, Mister Gay?"

"Never mind what it means."

"Well, I can't do games, Mister GAAAAAY... I have Cree."

"Cree?"

"Cree?'

"Cree?"

"Yes, I have cree cos I have the stress."

Mr Mental Evans stops sharpening his weapon of choice.

"Stress, boy... stress?"

"Yes, Mister Gaaaaay. My doctor said I was a bag of nerves."

Mr Mental Evans grabs him by collar

"Your nerves will be in a bag soon enough, boy."

"Hang on, Mister Mental-Evans... what do you mean a 'bag of nerves'? A bag of nerves, McAleer?"

"Why are you saying everything twice, Sir, saying everything twice?"

"Shut up, Dekka."

Mr Mental Evans growls

"Mister Pope gave me stress, Sir."

Mister Gay swings his hand by his groin

"Is it because of his abnormally big hanging ball bag?"

The two boys look confused at each other.

"No, Mister Gaaaaaaay, it's not because of his abnormally big hanging ball bag. Its cos of cross country runs."

"Cross country runs? Cross country runs?"

"Sir, you're saying everything twice again, saying everything twice. Twice."

"Shut it, I said, Dekka! Now, McAleer, why on earth would cross country runs give you stress?"

"Fear of things."

"What *things*?"

"Lions, Sir.

"LIONS!"

"And tigers, Sir."

"TIGERS!"

"And bears."

"Lions and tigers and bears?"

"Oh my!"

"Dekka, you're in enough trouble as it is. Smoking, bunking... womanising..."

"Womanising. Mister Gay? My spud gun isn't working yet, sir."

"I'll spud gun him now... arrgghhhh!"

Mr Mental-Evans starts twitching, sucking on oxygen mask likein the movie blue velvet

"McAleer, what are you on about... fear of lions, and tigers and bears?"

"OH MY!"

"Mister Mental-Evans, twist Dekka's nipple clean off."

"My pleasure..."

Mister Mental-Evans twists Dekka's nipple... Dekka screams

"Ooohhhhhh my nipple!!!"

"I get stress, Mister Gaaaaay ...in case they leap out on me."

"Who? Lions and tigers and bears?"

"Oh..."

Mr Mental-Evans stares at Dekka...

"It's not just them, Mister Gaaaaaay... other things like wild dogs and midgets... the drunks from the Park View..."

"I drink in the Park View."

"Sorry, Mister Mental-Evans... The Wyndham, I meant."

"I drink there, as well."

"No...no...no... I meant that place in Cardiff, where all the transsexuals go... 'Club X'."

"What do you know about 'Club X', boy?"

"Nothing, Mister Gaaaaay."

"It better be. Now stop all this stress nonsense."

"But I have a note, Mister Gaaaaaay."

"I don't care if you have a letter off your doctor."

"I *have* got a letter off my doctor."

"What does it say, boy?"

"It probably says he's got stress, Sir, stress, Sir... bloody hell I'm saying everything twice now, twice now."

"Quiet, Dekka."

Malachy pulls letter out of pocket and starts to read it in an Indian accent...

"It says: please excuse Malachy McAleer from any form of physical activity due to an acute and dangerous form of the stress... signed *(Pause)* Doctor Quirk."

"Doctor Quirk? That's not a real doctor's name."

"It is, Mister Mental-Evans."

"Pass it here, McAleer."

Malachy passes it to Mister Gay. He starts to read it in silence...

"Oh, you have got stress. OK, hold out your hand... six of the best will cure your stress."

"I can't Mister Gaaaaay... read the back."

Mister Mental-Evans snatches it off him and starts to read it out loud in his normal accent...

"And he can't even have six of the best..."

"Mister MENTAL-EVANS *(Mr Gay stops him reading)*... it's the same doctor."

"What?"

"It's the same doctor. You need to read it in the same accent as McAleer did."

"But... I can't do accents."

"Just do it Mister Mental-Evans."

Mr Mental-Evans coughs and starts reading the rest of the letter. He sounds more like a South African. Malachy and Dekka and Mister Gay start giggling...

"And he can't even have six of the best, OK, to cure his stress. Signed again, Doctor Quirk. *(pause)* PS. I am a real doctor."

He rolls up letter and throws it at Dekka

"Right, McAleer... this time you can go *(Mr Mental-Evans is speechless... both boys try and leave)* NOT you, DEKKA. You're having it large, boy."

"But Sir, I wasn't smoking."

"Calling me a liar, boy?"

"No, Mister Mental-Evans."

"You've been fighting, disturbing classes, causing Mr Hill to go off his rocker... bunking, stealing... and now smoking. What are we to do with you, boy?"

"I haven't been bunking, Mister Gay."

"And I thought that McAleer pikey boy was a bad influence on you. Now I'm not sure it's not the other way around."

"And I've never stole anything in my life."

"It's only a matter of time, boy... it's only a matter of time. And then God only knows what else it will lead to. Gambling, probably. And then pinching cars... and then womanising... and drugs. And a stretch in prison, just like your brother, I've been told. It must run in the family."

"But, he's not really in prison, Mister Gay. I just said that. He's really an IT Executive working in a computer company in Milton Keynes. My mother's really proud of him."

"An IT Executive!? Sewing mail bags more like."

"He is, Sir."

"A liar as well as a smoker."

"But, I'm not - and I don't smoke, Mister Gay."

"You don't smoke? You don't smoke? Smoking like a little chimney, I was told."

"But I wasn't, Mister Gay... honest."

"Oohh, so it's Mr Mental-Evans who's a liar then, is that what you are telling me, is it?"

"No, Mister Gay. OK, I was only trying it... I don't really smoke, honest."

"Boy, I can smell it on you - you smell like a disused tyre factory. Now, what are we going to do with you?"

"I won't do it again, Mister Gay... on my Mother's life."

"Don't ever say that, boy. It's not fair on your poor mother."

"But I won't... I promise..."

"Do you know the thing which frustrates me about boys like you?"

"When we smoke, Mister Gay?"

"Of course, when you smoke, boy, otherwise you wouldn't be here. Are you *trying* to be amusing?"

Silence

"Are you?"

"No, Mister Gay."

"Stop talking then. Now, where was I? Oh, I know... the thing what really frustrates me about boys like you, Dekka, is I've been told your grades are good - well, more than good: excellent, in fact. And, I hear you want to go to University?"

"Yes, Mister Gay, I do... I want to be Astronaut, to go to flying school in NASA in America..."

"Well, let me tell you now... NASA doesn't take students who fight, swear, bunk off..."

"I don't bunk off, Sir."

"Don't interrupt me, boy, when I'm giving you one of my life lesson lectures."

"Sorry, Sir."

"Sorry, *who*?"

"Sorry, Mister Gay."

"Well, NASA are not going to put up with a fighting, biting, swearing, suspender wearing, bunking, sulking, stealing, feeling, smoking, poking, joking, spotty, potty, gambling, ambling, titting, knitting, car pinching, cock inching, womanising, lying, glue sniffing, arse biffing, yobbo... now ARE they, Dekka? *(Silence) Are they*?"

"Sorry, Mister Gay, I must have dozed off... what did you say?"

"I'm not saying all that again. Anything to say for yourself before the punishment?"

Silence

Mr Mental-Evans gets a big vicious weapon ready...

"Look in to my eyes, not around the eyes."

"Are you *actually* mental, boy?"

"I'll pull his eyes out now, in a minute."

"Not yet, Mister Mental-Evans."

"Sorry, Mister Gay, it's my sense of humour."

"Sense of humour, is it? So, when Louie Armstrong was on the moon, did he do a little moon-dance while juggling tennis balls? Did he?"

Mister Mental Evans snaps his weapon shut. Makes a loud cracking noise. Dekka gulps.

"No gravity to juggle, Sir... and it wasn't Louie Armstrong... it was Neil."

Silence

"If you want to be funny, Dekka, go join the circus. Mister Mental-Evans... extract his two of his teeth."

"Teeth?!"

"Yesssss..."

"But, Sir."

Mr Mental-Evans moves in closer...

Phone rings... Mister Gay answers

"Oh my God, never mind him, Mister Mental-Evans, someone's set Mister Robert's hair on fire in the science lab!"

Both teachers go running out, Dekka walks out slowly touching his front teeth.

"Thank flying f...f...fish for that."

Schoolkids in the 70's were made out of skin, blood and desperation

JUNE 22nd 1976

Miss Chicken's class

9.20am

CAPONE

"Morning, Class."

"Morning, Miss Chicken."

"Cluck, cluck… cluck… cluck… cluck…"

Laughter

"Malachy, that wasn't funny the first time you did it, and it's not funny after the ninety ninth time… OK?"

"It is a *bit* funny, Miss."

"If you say so. Now, everyone take your seats on this beautiful, fine, sunny morning."

They all shuffle into position.

Mrs Chicken starts singing

"Hey, Miss..."

"Yes, Mary Jones?"

"Why are you looking so happy today?"

"Am I?"

"You are, Miss, you look like you have just won the pools."

"My grandad won the pools... six million big ones he won. Lives in LA now... next to Steve Austin...."

"Shut up, Jenkins."

"He does, Dekka!"

"What, your grandad won six million pounds and he now he actually lives next door to the six-million-dollar man? How spooky is that?"

"Yep, he does. And Elvis Presley lives the other side! I'll bring a photo in tomorrow."

"Jenkins, even for you that's quite a tall little story. Now, be quiet."

"But, Miss?"

"Quiet, Jenkins."

Laughter

"Ha ha, Jenkins... even Miss knows you're lying."

"It's not a lie, Dekka. I have a..."

"Yeah, we know - you have a photo and you will bring it in tomorrow, but you never do."

"You two... quiet, I said."

Silence

"Miss... so... why are you looking so happy?"

"Well, class can you keep a secret?"

"Is it about Mister Pope, Miss?"

"What, Malachy? What about Mister Pope?"

"About him knocking Miss Foley, the cookery teacher, off? Cos if it is, it ain't a secret anymore... everyone knows about it."

"He's right, Miss... my postman told my mother about it, then my mother told the rest of my street. She's got a mouth like Portsmouth; my father always says."

"Did she now, Jenny? That's very naughty of her. But, no... it's not about Mister Pope."

"It's news about me."

"Oh no, you ain't dying are you, Miss? Oh no... don't die, please."

"Don't worry, Hannah, I'm not dying... don't cry."

Hannah starts to sob...

"But, the last time my father said he had news for me, Miss, it was about our Cat, Alf... and then he died."

105

"Who died? The cat or your father?"

"Alf, Dekka. Alf died. Tell him, Miss?"

"Behave, Dekka. It's OK, Hannah, I have good news about me, not bad news. Honest."

"You are leaving?"

Loud ooohhhh from the class

"Sometimes I wish I was, Malachy... but sadly for you, and for me, I'm not. The good news is everyone... I'm getting married."

Ooohhhh from the girls

Uugghhhh from the boy.

"Is that all? Thought you were going to tell us something really exciting..."

"Like what, Carl Cross?"

"Something... like... like you were gonna go rock climbing up the Keyhole Cave... or go on Blue Peter."

Laughter

"I agree, it's not as exciting as going on Blue Peter, Carl, but it's exciting to me."

"I'm really excited for you, Miss."

"Thank you, Marie Jones."

"And me, Miss Chicken."

"Thank you too, Hannah."

Silence

"Are you up the duff then, Miss."

"Malachy, NO. I'm not up the d – pregnant."

"Are you sure?"

"I'm positive. That's a terrible thing to say..."

"It's not, Miss. Everyone in my family that gets married are normally pregnant."

"And mine."

"And mine."

"And mine."

"And mine."

"And mine."

"And mine."

"Me, too."

"Well, class... I hate to disappoint you all, but I'm definitely *not* having a baby."

Silence

"If you did have a baby, Miss..."

Silence

"Yessssssss, Malachy... continue!"

"If you did have a baby... would you have it like other women do?"

"What do you mean?"

"Like normal women... or would you lay an egg first?"

Laughter

"See, Miss... egg... chicken... chicken... egg!"

"I get it, Malachy... and since I'm in a good mood, I'll leave you off with that one - just this once. Now, let's get some work done."

"Miss? Miss?

"Yes, Marie Jones?"

"Who are you marrying, then?"

"Well, Marie... he's..."

"Is he Big Ken, the gangster, Miss? I heard he's getting married."

"No, Carl Cross, it is not Big Ken the gangster. And why would I want to marry Big Ken the gangster?"

"To be Big Ken the gangster's Moll, ain't it? Would be miles better than being a boring teacher."

"Thank you, Carl. Maybe next time."

"I'd love to be a gangster's moll, Miss."

"Jenny Phillips... now why on *earth* would you want to be a moll?

"It sounds so glamourous... all romantic like. Imagine walking into a posh hotel in Ponty, on the arm of Al Capri."

Laughter

"It's Al *Capone*, you idiot. Not Al Capri."

"Don't call me an idiot, Dekka. I'm not an idiot, RIGHT. I'M NOT AN IDIOT. Tell him, Miss."

"Ok, Jenny, cool down. He was only messing and... and do me a favour, put your jumper back on."

"But Miss, I'm hot..."

"I can see that, and so can everyone else. Frankie, stop dribbling."

"Mmmm dribble...Mmmm dribble...Mmmm penis."

"Just do as I say, Jenny."

Silence

"Is your boyfriend good looking, Miss?"

"Hannah, he's very good looking... like a Hollywood actor."

"What's his name?"

"His name is Pete Green, Marie Jones."

"He doesn't *sound* like a Hollywood actor. Sounds more like a character from Cluedo... Pete Green did it in the library with a candlestick..."

"Yeah, yeah... very amusing, Dekka."

"I have my moments, Miss."

"And what does he do, Miss?"

"If you must know, Marie Jones, he is a..."

"MISS, MISS, don't tell us!"

"Why not, Dekka?"

"Let us try and guess, it will be a laugh. Come on, please? We can get everyone in the class to have a go. Please??"

"Yes, come on, Miss, that will be great...

"Ok, but nothing stupid."

All the class seem excited. They all start thinking.

"OK, since it's your idea, Dekka, you can go first."

Silence

"Is he a builder?"

"No."

"Is he a cowboy, Miss?

"She said nothing stupid, Crossy..."

"Being a cowboy ain't stupid. John Wayne ain't stupid, he's famous, isn't he, Miss?"

"Yes, Carl, he is."

"YESSS. I was right. He's a cowboy... he's a cowboy. Can I meet him, Miss? Please? Please?"

"No, Carl. I was talking about John Wayne being famous. My boyfriend is not a cowboy, sorry."

"Is he a Mexican bandit, then?"

"Crossy, you can't have another go."

"I can, Dekka. Can't I Miss?"

"No, Carl... let the others have a go, first."

"Oh, OK."

"Is he a French poet, and writes you love poems every day?"

"That's sick."

"It's not sick, Malachy... its very nice, but sadly Jenny, he's not a French Poet. But he is very romantic."

"Oh, that's nice, Miss."

Gagging sound from Malachy.

"Malachy, do you want go outside?"

"Yes, please."

"Well, you are not. Christine Lee... what do you think?"

"Umm... is he a maths teacher, Miss Chicken."

Laughter

"Christine, are you obsessed with maths teachers?"

"No, Dekka."

"He's not a Maths Teacher, but good guess."

"Is he a porn star, Miss?"

"Frankie, I'm not even going to answer that."

"Oh!"

"Miss... what's a porn star?"

"Nevermind, Hannah. What about you, Jenkins? What do you think he is?"

"A fireman like my Uncle Joe. Best fireman in the country, Miss. He put of a massive burning building by himself and saved ninety-seven lives last week."

"He didn't, Jenkins."

"He did, Marie Jones, so there. He was in the paper, won a medal. I'll bring a photo in tomorrow."

"Not quite, Jenkins... but you are close."

A baffled Ooohhhh from the class

"Ohhhh, he's something like a fireman..."

Monkey noises

"Cool down, Cross. Stop getting so excited.,"

"But oohhh... ohhhhh... Miss, is he is... he a... a..."

"Is he an arsonist, Miss?"

Laughter

"No, Malachy. He's not an arsonist."

"Well, he must be a gardener then."

"Dekka, am I missing something here? How is a gardener like a fireman?"

"Well, my old man says that firemen are lazy so-and-so's who sleep all night and do gardening in the day."

"Oh, I haven't heard that, but no... he's not."

"Arrrggghhhhhhh!"

"What's wrong, Malachy?"

"Don't tell me, Miss?"

"Don't tell you what, Malachy?"

"Don't tell me he's a... he's a... pig."

"A what?"

"A policeman, Miss... please no."

"In fact, he is."

"Oh, no...you can't marry a pig."

"Malachy, stop calling him that, and I am marrying a police man... a year next August, in Saint Mary's Church."

"Well, me and Dekka ain't coming to the wedding then, Miss... not if he's a pig."

"Oh, I'm so sorry to hear that Malachy... because we wanted you to be our best man."

"Yeah, right."

Laughter

"OK, class... let's get some work done, now. Books out, turn to page...'

"Miss, oohh, Miss, oohhh..."

"What is it, Carl?

"Is he Kojak, Miss?"

Laughter

"Miss Chicken?"

"What, Malachy?"

"Who luvs you baby?"

Miss Chicken bursts out laughing. The rest of the class join in.

Feb 9th 1978

Miss Chicken's class

11am

MINGIN'

"Miss? Miss?"

"Quiet Jenny... carry on with the test."

Silence

"But, Miss, there's a weird person in the yard. Look!"

Everyone gets up and moves to the window

"Oh, God. She's mingin', Miss."

"Everyone get back in your seats this instant."

"But she looks piss - drunk, Miss."

"Malachy..."

"But she can hardly walk."

"My father walks like that most nights, Miss. Piles like blood oranges."

"Too much information, Hannah. Now, sit down everyone."

"My mother puts lard on 'em for him, Miss. I had to do it last night" *(she sniffs her fingers)*

"I bet Miss Foley does the same with Mister Pope's plums."

Laughter

"Quiet, Malachy."

"Mmmm... plums... Mmmm lard... Mmmm penis."

"Cool down, Frankie."

"What if she sets up camp in the yard, imagine that. 'Drunk woman lives on hockey field'."

"She won't, Dekka."

"That's disgusting. Where would she go to the toilet?"

"She'll shit behind the posts, Jenny."

"Malachy!"

"I'm only saying... that's where I would go."

"I'm not playing hockey again if that drunk woman does her business by the posts."

116

"She won't, Jenny, she probably belongs in some home. Now, come on... away from the window."

They all take their seats, Maria stands alone...

"Miss?"

"I said quiet, Maria Jones, and sit down."

"But, Miss... can I leave please?"

"No, you're in the middle of a test."

"Maybe she's an IRA terrorist..."

"Why on God's earth would she be an IRA terrorist, Dekka??"

"Oh my God, she's going to blow us up. MISSSSS!!!"

"She's *not,* Hannah... get up from under your desk."

"They come in all shapes and sizes, Miss. Look at Bobby Sands... he's thin as a rake."

"What are you on about, Dekka?"

"She's here to bomb the school..."

"I had an uncle who was a..."

"Shut up Jenkins. Whatever you were going to say, don't say it."

"But, Miss..."

Malachy whacks the desk... they all scream and jump

"Now, Dekka, why would an IRA terrorist... bomb a *Catholic* school?"

"Cos she's piss-drunk, Miss."

"I'm warning you, Malachy..."

"Oh no*,* we are all going to die."

Hannah does sign of the cross

"SHUT UP, SHUT UP... *(They all look at Maria Jones standing by the window)* She's not an IRA terrorist, or mad, and she's not going to set up camp on the hockey field."

"How do you know?"

"Cos' Jenny, she's my mother, right. Cos she's my drunken, alcoholic mother, Miss. I've got to go."

Maria runs out... silence falls

"Miss?"

"Not now, Jenny."

"But Miss... Maria Jones's drunken alcoholic mother is actually having a poo on the hockey field..."

They all run to window

"And she's wiping her bum on the posts."

Feb 9th 1978

School Yard

1pm

LUVS

Dekka walks over to Maria in the schoolyard

"You ok, Maria Jones?"

"What do you think, Dekka?"

"I'm sorry about taking the mickey out of your mother, I... didn't know. None of us did." (*Silence)* Is she...better, today?"

"If 'better' means her lying in bed in her own vomit and me making my own dinner and ironing my school uniform, and cleaning the house and making myself breakfast this morning... then, yes... she's fine."

"Sorry."

"Just talk about something else."

"But..."

"Something else... please."

"I was wondering if you...if you...ever fancy...fancy, going...going... *(silence - she looks at him)* Humm...Hum...if you ever fancy...going...you know, arrgghhhh out on a...on a...on a..."

Malachy runs towards them...

"Why don't you two get married?"

"What?"

"You'll be writing her name on your satchel next... 'Dekka luvs Maria Jones'. Hey, Maria Jones, your mother's one crazy lady...is she always that drunk?"

Maria runs off crying

"Malachy, you idiot. Why did you say that?"

"What? You two should get married?"

"No, about her mother. You, more than anyone, should know better with what your dad does to you."

'Oh, he's not my dad... he's my *step*dad. Get it fuckin' right."

The boys stare at each other, fists clenched

March 14th 1978

Corridor

11am

COUGH

In the corridor... Dekka, Malachy and Frankie are standing outside a the nurse's room.

"Right, whoever gets thrown out without her doing it, wins *(counts on in his hand)* twenty-five pence."

"Easy, Malachy."

"But I want her to do it to me. Mmmmm."

"You're a weirdo, Frankie."

"Thanks, Dekka....Mmmm penis."

"Right, I'm going in."

"Good luck, Dekka, good luck."

Dekka knocks on the door and enters room… the strict looking nurse is putting on rubber gloves

"Trousers off."

"Ain't you going to buy me dinner first, Nurse?"

"What?"

"Nothing."

The nurse places her hands on his balls

"Cough."

Silence

"Cough, I said."

"Why?"

"Because I need to check you."

"For what?"

"Make sure everything is working, down there."

"Like a toaster?"

Nurse laughs.

"If you put it like that, yes, like a toaster. I need to check it's toasting your… bread.

Now, cough."

"My uncle touches it, Nurse. He's always touching it."

"What does he do?"

"I don't want to talk about it."

"You can tell me... I'm qualified!"

"Can you do electrics as well then?"

"What?"

"My toaster... my uncle blew it up see. Stuck a knife in it."

"Oh, a *real* toaster. That's ok then... and no, I can't fix it."

"Why did you say you could then?"

"Never mind... just give me a little cough."

Dekka makes a strange throaty sound

"I can't cough."

"You can't cough?"

"I can't cough."

"You can't cough?"

"I can't cough when I'm nervous."

"There's nothing to be nervous about..."

"Nurse, you've got your hand on my toaster."

A boy races in, scared... he looks about...

"Hide me please...I only broke a hacksaw blade in Metalwork...I didn't...I didn't mean it."

We hear a chainsaw. Mr Mental-Evans appears. He chases boy out through door. Dekka turns to the nurse.

"What if I give you a little laugh, instead?"

"No...you need to cough."

"I can't."

"What's your name?"

"Dekka, nurse. Johnny Dekka."

"Did your brother go to this school... Royston?"

"I haven't got a brother. I haven't even got any parents...adopted. Lived the life of an orphan..."

"Oh...I'm so sorry to hear that."

"Why? Did you know them."

"Who?"

"My parents."

"No, sorry."

"Are they black?"

"What?"

"Are my parents black?"

"No...they're not black."

"Argghhh...so you *do* know them. What are they like? I need to know. Is my mother pretty? Does my father work on the buses? Have they got a dog...I bet they have...a golden Labrador...Alun, I bet his name is?"

"I don't know them; I just want you to cough."

"I miss them. **(sobs) (silence)** I've never met them...but I miss them so much. Maaaaammmmm... daaaaadddd... Alllluuuunn... my... black parents' dog."

"Please, just cough."

"I'll try."

"Let me get my fingers back in the right positions...right...go on."

'Nurse, I can't. Your little moustache is putting me off."

"WHAT?!"

"You ain't a man, are you?"

"NO!"

"My parents always warned me about letting strange men with moustaches touch my privates."

"Get out. GET OUT - hang on... you said you didn't know your parents!!"

"Not my *real* parents...jokin' ones...like Crossy's eggs."

"You are insane, just get out, now. Go...and send in the next pupil, FRANKIE PRATT."

Silence, then Frankie sneaks up behind the nurse, his trousers down

"Mmmm… toast. Mmmm… cough… Mmmm… penis."

Nurse screams

April 19th 1978

Main assembly hall

1.30pm

BAMBER

Parents / Teachers meeting: Sister Flip and Sister Flop and Miss Chicken sitting in the centre of the room. Miss Chicken's drinking from hip flask, the nuns are smoking, they're relaxing. Dekka's parents walk towards Miss Chicken. Miss Chicken spies them...

"Quick there's another two."

The nuns shuffle off to the back of the room, where they start playing rock, paper, stone, scissors

"Mister and Mrs Dekka, isn't it?"

"Yes."

They all sit down.

"I'm Johnny's form tutor, Miss Chicken."

Father starts laughing at her name. Miss Chicken stares at him.

"How's he's doing?"

"Well, Mrs Dekka, he's a very bright boy… but he's got a habit of not taking things seriously…"

Mother and teacher look at father, who's still giggling. He stops laughing. In background, the nuns sit on the edge of the stage and start eating Curly Wurlys

"We both know which side of the family he gets that from, don't we June?"

"Here we go… what now Bernard?"

"Her family, Miss Ostrich, are a bit odd."

"My family aren't odd?"

"Not odd? Not odd? Your Aunty Ethel ran away to join the bloody circus when she was forty-seven."

"She's a cook! She wasn't getting fired from a bloody canon."

"No, that's your Uncle Alan, the midget."

"Excuse me…can we get back to Johnny please?"

"Oh, sorry, Miss. Oh, look at me, calling you Miss… it's like I'm back in bloody school."

"Bernard…stop swearing."

"Johnny does need to knuckle down and concentrate more."

"Her family, *again*."

"My family? My family? Your brother thinks he's Richie Valance - but with dirty fingernails. And don't get me started on your mother..."

"June, I warned you before, don't you *dare* say anything about my mother. She brought four of us up after my father buggered off with the pools man. We lived in a two up two down house, with no running water...rats like cats. Three jobs she had...three bloody jobs. One in Op's, one in Thorns and other in Keyser Bonder. We had no money, but lots of poor-quality broken biscuits. No electric, but... thousands of 40-watt bulbs... and...and...and all the bras we could eat."

"Bernard, no one cares about your bloody mother."

"Mr and Mrs Dekka...we haven't got much time left..."

"See, June. You've upset Miss Ostrich, now. Carry on love."

"Chicken. It's Miss Chicken. Idiot."

"That's what I said."

"Anyway... look, if Johnny wants to follow his dream and go to University...."

"UNI BLOODY VERSITY..."

"Yes, Mister Dekka."

"I know he's challenged, but he's no Bamber Gascoigne."

"To become an Astronaut."

"AN ASTRO BLOODY NAUT. Are you mental?"

"Stop swearing, Bernard."

"Mister Dekka, I'm not mental, I'm a geography teacher."
"OX-bow soup lakes."

"And I thought the fucking pupils were dull... **(Miss Chicken thought to herself. Back to the parents...)** Jonny wants to be an Astronaut, but I think with his vivid imagination, he could be a writer."

"A writer? A writer? He wrote a note to the milk man last Tuesday: we ended up with fifteen pints of milk, four dozen eggs...and three blue movies on Betamax. The milkman doesn't even sell eggs."

"But Mister Chicken, we want our Johnny to follow in his brother's footsteps...we're so proud of Royston."

"I don't think going to prison is anything to be proud of, do you, Mrs Dekka?"

"PRISON?! Who's in bloody prison?"

"Relax, June..."

"Shut it, Bernard. Now, Miss Chicken, who's in prison?"

"Your oldest boy... 'Razorblade Dekka'."

"I'll bloody kill him... I'll strangle him when I get home."

"So, your oldest son *didn't* rob the chemist shop for drugs?"

"The chemist bloody shop?"

"Then the Spar shop, for drink?"

'The Spar bloody shop?'

"And then Harry, the butcher?"

"Harry the Butchers??"

"For sausages?"

"Royston's a bloody vegetarian!"

"Then… why did he rob Harry the Butcher?"

"HE BLOODY DIDN'T! He's an IT executive, working in Milton Keynes. Come on, Bernard we're going home."

"And he's just brought a brand new, second hand Capri…one careful female owner…two tone. That's the car - not the female owner!"

"Come on, Bernard."

"I did say, Mrs Dekka…that Jonny has a very vivid imagination…"

"I'll give him vivid imagination."

"Goodnight, Miss Hen."

"It's chicken, idiot."

"Goodnight, Miss Chicken-idiot."

Catholics can't sing the blues

April 26th 1978

Miss Chicken's class

9am

GLASS

Miss Chicken walks into the class with new boy... there is a loud Ooohhhh from the rest of the class.

"Good morning, class... *(they shuffle in their seats)* Now, everyone...this is a new pupil, Ralph. Ralph Bracegirdle."

"Miss, that's can't be his real name. It sounds like a spy's name."

"What, Malachy?"

"Ooooo is he a spy, Miss?"

"No, Hannah. I don't think so."

"How do you know he's not a spy, Miss?"

"Because, Maria Jones, he's twelve years old…and his mother just dropped him off in a Morris Minor."

"I'm thirteen."

"What, Ralph?"

"I was thirteen last week."

Another loud Ooohhhh from the class.

"OK…but, that's still too young to be a spy."

"I'd like to be a spy, Miss."

"I thought you wanted to be a cowboy, Crossy?"

"I do, but I wanna be a spy as well, Jenny."

"A… cowspy?"

"No, Maria Jones, I ain't gonna spy on cows. That's boring."

"Oh no…I've forgot: I've got crabs."

"*What*, Hannah??"

All the class move their chairs away from her.

"I got them off some boy in Porthcawl. *(Hannah pulls a dead crab out of her bag)* See, crab."

"Miss…Miss…"

"Quiet, Malachy."

"Arrgghhh! What's wrong with Ralph's eye? He's like a baddie from a James Bond movie??"

"Do you want to go see Mister Gay, Carl Cross?"

"To tell him Ralph looks like a baddie from a James Bond film??"

"No, Carl...to tell him that you are being very rude."

"I could be a Bond girl..."

"Not now, Jenny."

'Mmmm... pussy... Mmmm... galooooorrrrree.... Mmmm... penis.'

"And you Frankie."

Silence

"It's glass."

"Miss, Ralph just said something."

"It's made of glass."

"Miss...he said his eye is made of glass."

"I heard him, Maria Jones."

A huge loud Ooohhhh from the class.

"Why?"

"Malachy...quiet."

"I'm only asking. You always say we should ask about stuff."

"Was he born with it?"

"Of course, he wasn't born with it, Hannah."

"Did the Russians pull it out with a spoon? When they caught him spying, Miss?"

"Quiet, Cross."

"My uncle had two glass eyes, once..."

"No, he didn't, Jenkins."

"He did, Maria Jones, so there. Two, big, blue, glass eyes... and one plastic ear, actually."

"Hang on... last week you said your uncle climbed Everest?"

"He did, Dekka."

"What? Your Uncle climbed Everest with two glass eyes?"

"And one plastic ear. I have a photo of him on the top holding a flag... I'll bring it in tomorrow."

"Like balls he did."

"Malachy, stop swearing."

"But, Miss, he's talking bollocks again."

"MALACHY!"

'Arrggghhhhhh... get off me."

"Carl Cross... leave Ralph alone!"

"But, Miss... his glass eye is staring at me."

"It's. *He's* not staring at you."

"It is... look... it's staring straight at me when I stand here. *(Carl runs about the room)* It's staring at me by here, as well."

"Quiet, Cross. Now, everyone get your history books out. Chapter five, Mary Queen of Scots... I'll be back in five minutes. Malachy... not a word."

"But..."

"*Not* a word."

Door opens... door closes

Silence

Malachy rushes over to Ralph's desk

"Oh...you... Ralph the spy with the glass eye..."

"Malachy, don't call him that."

"Shut up, Jenny big knockers."

"Mmmm... door. Mmmm... stops. Mmmmm... penis."

"Arrrgghh... stop staring at me, Frankie! Anyway, I'm going to be a page three model when I'm sixteen...you'll see Ralph."

"Not with his left eye, he won't."

Everyone laughs, except Ralph

"That's cruel, Malachy."

"Can I touch them, Jenny? Mmmmmmmm."

"No, Frankie...stop staring."

"Mmmm. Mellllloooons."

Ralph starts crying

"Look, you've made him cry now."

"I'm not crying. I'm drooooling, Mmmm... penis."

"No, not you Frankie...the one-eyed spy boy...look."

Silence

Sobbing

"Are there any tears coming out of it?"

"I'll check now, Malachy."

"No, Crossy."

"Shut up, Marie Jones."

"Get off...get off..."

Crossy and Ralph start to struggle... Malachy helps...

"Hold his hands down."

"I have Malachy."

Struggle continues...

"Come on, Ralph... let's have a peek."

"Malachy... leave him alone!"

"Shut up, Dekka... come and help us."

"Arrgghhhhhhhhhhhhh."

"Malachy, get your fingers out of Ralph's eye! You'll blind him!"

"Shut up, Maria Jones. Hold his hands tighter, Crossy."

"Arrrggghhhhhhhhhhh..."

"Let him go, Malachy!"

"Dekka... stop pulling me!"

"Well, get off him!"

"I've nearly got it..."

Dekka and Maria pull Malachy off.

Crash.

Bang.

Wallop.

POP.

Roll.

Silence

"Look what you done now, Dekka."

"You done it, Malachy"'

"ARRRRRRGGGHHHHH!!! ARRRRRRGGGGGGHHHH!!"

"Jenny, stop screaming!"

"ARRRGGGGH Look, Maria Jones... his eye, it's gone.!"

"My eye... my eye... I've lost my eye!"

Crossy covers is own eye and runs about

"Not *your* eye, Crossy. Ralph's eye's gone... look!"

Silence.

"ARRGGGGGGHHHHHHHHHHHH!!! ARRRGGGGGHHHHHHHH!!"

"Will everyone STOP screaming!"

"Look at Dekka, thinking he's in charge."

"Malachy, I'm warning you..."

"He looks so scary."

"I can see his brain!"

"You can't, Crossy."

"I'm sure I can."

More screams...

"Never mind that, we've got to find his eye quickly, before Chicken gets back!"

"Everyone: on their hands and knees."

Chairs scraping the floor... lots of shuffling about...

"I've found it, I've found it!"

"Well done, Hannah. Give it to me, quick."

"Here it is, Dekka."

"Watch you don't drop it."

Dekka holds it up like the famous scene from the 'Lion King'

"This isn't his eye... it's a gob-stopper! Arrghhh... it's all sticky."

"I'll have that..."

Jenkins takes it and puts it in his mouth

More screams...

"Arrggghhh, Jenkins... it's got all hair on it!"

"Right - find the proper eye!"

"Oh, look at Captain Dekka and his girlfriend here...giving out all the orders."

"If it wasn't for you, Malachy...we wouldn't be in this mess."

Silence

"I've got it...arrghhhhh its cold."

"Pass it here, Crossy."

"I wonder if it bounces."

"NO, Crossy!"

Silence has he hands it over…

"Now, Ralph… come out of the corner… take your hands from your face. Here goes… good as new."

Screams

"It's the wrong way around…it's all white!"

"He really looks like a baddie in a Bond film!"

"I'm going to be a Bond girl…"

"Yeah, Danny Bond's girl. Ralph stop fighting me…let me just…get it out…I can't move it."

"Hannah, where's that crab?"

Hannah hands Dekka the crab…

Ralph screams.

"No, Ralph…it's ok…I'm not going to use a crab. It's coming…its coming… *(POP)* I've got it!"

Door opens…

"Johnny Dekka… what are you doing?"

"I'm trying to pop Ralph's glass eye back in."

"Put the eye on my desk and get out. I'll deal with you later."

"But…"

"NOW!"

"Thanks, Malachy."

Dekka storms out

"What did I do?"

Slugs and sport teachers have the same DNA

June 23rd 1978

Miss Chicken's class

2.34pm

SASQUATCH

"Carl Cross...you're the only one not to have paid up for the school trip to Bristol Zoo."

Silence

"Well?"

"I don't want to go, Miss."

A loud Ooohhhh noise for the class

"You do, Crossy."

"I don't, Hannah."

"Come on, it will be a craic. If we're lucky, we can steal a monkey."

"Malachy, you better not steal anything. In fact, you are lucky to be going after the incident with Mr Price's organ."

"Don't you mean Mrs Price's *piano*, Miss?"

"NO, Maria Jones. I mean Mister Price's *organ*."

"Mmmm... piano... Mmmm... organ... Mmmm... penis."

"Quiet, Frankie."

"I didn't touch it, Miss."

"Malachy... they found the superglue in your bag."

"I was framed."

"I bet. Now, Carl... I need to know if you coming or not?"

"I'm not."

"But you love monkeys. And there's loads of monkeys there...gorillas, chimps...orangeee u-tanees..."

"I don't anymore, Hannah."

"Doris the dinner lady be there."

"Dekka, that's not funny."

"But she does looks like sasquatch, Miss."

Laughter

"Maria Jones, the poor lady can't help it."

"Having a shave now and again, would help."

Laughter

"Mmmm… shave… Mmmm… hairy. Mmmm… penis."

Laughter

"Now, Carl… last chance… Bristol Zoo or not. *(Silence)* It's only five pounds."

Carl gets up and kicks chair across the room.

"I haven't got five pounds. We haven't got any money. We had to hid behind the settee from the Leccy man last night… my mother can't even get anything on tic anymore from the shop."

"Where are you going?"

"Home. I'm going home."

Door opens… and slams shut

Silence

"Miss… Miss."

"Not now, Malachy."

"But, Miss…"

"I said, shut up."

Malachy walks up to desk and slams a five pound note on it

"That's for Crossy's trip."

Malachy walks to the door

"Where did you get that from, Mal'?"

"Let's just say, Marie Jones, my stepfather won't be winning the four fifteen at Epson or getting his twenty woodbine tonight."

He walked out.

May 10th 1978

Mrs Gay's office

9am

PENGUIN

The day after the school trip: the two nuns march Dekka, Crossy Jenkins and Malachy into Mr Gay's office. Mental-Evans is already there with his suitcase. Mister Gay is pacing. Never a good sign.

"Right, you lot. There's only one word I'm going to say to you all **(pause)** *Peng...uin.*"

"Penguin?"

"Penguin, McAleer."

"Penguin?"

"Penguin, Dekka!"

"Penguin?"

"Peng... uin, Jenkins!"

"Isn't that two words, Mister Gay?"

"Stop being so thick, Cross."

"A pick up...a...pick up a...penguin."

"This is not a laughing matter, Dekka. Now... where is it?"

"Where's what, Mister Gay?"

"The penguin, boy. The penguin, boy?"

"What penguin boy? I never saw a penguin boy. What cage was he in, Sir?"

"Not a *penguin boy*, Cross...you inbred. Just a penguin, boy... there's a comma in it."

"A what, Sir?"

"A Pick up...pick up a... peng..."

"Dekka...say that again, and you will be beaten to within an inch of your sorrowful life and then expelled from school for ever...understand?"

Mr Mental-Evans growls like a cat.

Silence.

"UNDERSTAND!?"

"Yes, Mister Gay."

"Black eye... fighting again, McAleer?"

"My stepfather won on the horses, well kind of, last week... and took it out on me."

"I don't blame him. Where's the penguin?"

"I love chocolate biscuits, me, sir...but we can never afford real ones...we have jokin' ones."

"Shut up Cross. Now, someone from Bristol Zoo called this morning to say one of their penguins was missing..."

"Nothing to do with us, Mister Gay."

"Lying, Dekka! Now, tell me before Mister Mental-Evans goes to work on you lot."

"Let me at them... let me at them!"

"Maybe that polar bear ate it?"

"Polar bears don't eat penguins, Dekka."

"No, sir, they eat glazier mints."

"Cross... you are thicker than Doris the Dinner-lady's custard."

"My uncle fought a polar bear down the Brandy Bridge, once. Knocked him out in round three."

"Mister Mental-Evans... put Jenkins to sleep."

Mr Mental-Evans hits Jenkins with a bat across the head. Jenkins falls on floor.

"Before the police get involved... *where* is the bloody penguin?"

Mister Pope comes running in holding a box...

"It's OK... we've found it."

"Thank Ronnie Regan for that."

Mr Gay and Mental Evans and the nuns go and look at it

"Mister Pope... that is a cat, you retard."

"Are you sure, Mister gay? It's penguin colour."

"So is Sister Flip and Sister Flop... you idiot... It's got a bushy tail and a name on its collar."

"Ziggy."

On the other side of the room.

"I told you not to pinch it, Dekka."

"But, Crossy wanted it..."

"Yeah, I've never had a penguin before."

"None of us have had a bloody penguin before. Where is it now, Crossy?"

"It's a... a... a little bit dead."

"A little bit... *dead*?"

"OK, a lot dead. It froze to death."

"It's a penguin, Crossy... how the hell could it freeze to death??"

"I put it in the freezer before I went to bed, Dekka. When I woke up this morning... it was hard like a lolly pop. My sister was licking it, watching Bill and Ben."

"A real-life p... p... pppp... penguin."

"What we going to do?? We'll get expelled. I'll never be a cowboy then??"

"And no Astronaut College for me."

"I'll sort it."

Malachy turns around and shouts out.

"Mister Gaaaaaaay! I stole it. I stole the penguin, boy!"

"I knew it... bloody Pikeys! Where is it, McAleer?"

"I sold it."

"Sold it!? It's not a fucking carpet!"

"To Elwyn... the drug dealer."

"Elwyn, the drug dealer!?"

"He wanted to make a waist coat out of it."

Everyone in the room repeats the same thing

"Elwyn the drug dealer, wanted to make a waist coat out of the penguin you stole from Bristol zoo??"

"To go with his snake skinned boots..."

Everyone in the room repeats the same thing

"Elwyn the drug dealer, wanted to a make a waist coat out of the penguin you stole from Bristol zoo to go with his..."

"Stop it...stop it, for fuck sake. Malachy, you're in big, big trouble."

"But, sir..."

"The others had nothing to do with it, Mister Gay...honest."

Mister Mental-Evans stares into their faces...

"I don't believe them...they're all guilty."

"I agree, Mister Mental Evans. Now, take them down to the dungeon...and release the gimp priest. We'll see who is telling the truth."

Down in the basement... they were about to get tortured... but Carl Cross cracked within five minutes. They were all suspended for 2 months.

THE END OF YEAR ONE

WHERE ARE THEY NOW –
SCHOOL YEAR BOOK

Jonny Dekka... obviously did not become an astronaut, or the title of the book wouldn't have made any sense. But, he did take two pieces of advice off his best mate, Malachy. Firstly, he did marry Maria Jones and secondly, he did become a Writer. Maybe you have read some of his stuff!!!

Malachy McAleer... disappeared off the face of the earth in year three and was never, ever seen again. Many rumours circulated outside the tuck shop, that he became an Irish street fighter or a Colombian drug dealer or a goat herder living near Deri... but who knows? He could just be sitting next to you as you read this.

Carl 'Crossy' Cross... his dream came true when he became a cowboy with his firm 'Crossy's Cowboy Builders'. They specialise in roofs, walls and guttering. He also built a zoo at the bottom of his garden in Galon Uchaf, but got fined when a large cat escaped and bit a postman, and nicked a police car.

Maria Jones... married Dekka and became a Scriptwriter for 'The IT Crowd' and also for the 'Game of Thrones'. She makes a lovely chicken curry, too.

Hannah Price... achieved her goal of working in the Wimpy, but she didn't actually get to make any milkshakes. Although, she is still going to night school to help her achieve her ambition (but she maybe in the wrong class)!

Christine Lee... unbelievably, her life went into spiral after she left school. She turned to drink and drugs and even sold her body to old men driving Hillman Imps. It was tragic. Only messing! In reality, she passed all of her exams, went to university, and did become a maths teacher. She is single, and has 7 cats.

Frankie Pratt... beceme a priest and set up his very own church: The Church of the Untouched Penis. The Pope (not Mister Pope) often calls him up for a chat.

Colin Jenkins... became an MP for the Rhondda, and to this day still threatens to bring photos of his family's achievements in for everyone to see. He recently voted to bring back hanging, the black plague, and for poor people to work as 'toilet warmers' for richer people.

Jenni Cabbage... did become a beauty queen when she won 'Miss Pant Fish shop 1991'. She still walks around B&M's wearing her crown and sash, and smells of cod.

Ralph Bracegirdle... believe it or not, was actually a spy working for the CIA when he was 13 up until he took voluntary redundancy in 2013 (after losing his good eye in a strange boating accident on the Taff near Ponty).

Mister Gay... retired from the teaching profession in 1998, and sadly died in 2012. But, in between he was responsible for inventing many TV shows that mainly aired in Japan which involved various forms of torture and humiliation.

Mister Hill... is still in a 'cold dark place for teachers who suffer from post-teaching depression'. On the plus side, he is very good at painting birds and twigs.

Mister Pope… was sacked in Dekka's second year at Bishop J.R Hartley High School after he was caught in the girl's changing room, wearing some poor girl's bra and knickers. To be fair to him though, he still had that shuttlecock in place. He now works at DFS.

Mister Mental-Evans… retired in 1999 and went to work for the Samaritans. He has won 'Employee of the Year' six times whilst also becoming a published author with his novel about Nazis and their fluffy pets.

Miss Chicken… got married to her Policeman boyfriend and became Mrs Cockring - which of course did not help her situation as a teacher. In the end, she gave up and settled down to being a housewife and had two kids. And no, she didn't have them by laying eggs (real ones nor false ones).

Sister Flop and Sister Flip… left the school and became professional tag team wrestlers, winning 68 of their 69 professional fights. The only one they lost was to two four-feet-one druid sisters from Bala. In 2011, Sister Flop passed away while sunbathing down the Mumbles. Sister Flip gave up being a nun after that and is now a part time fruit machine repairman.

Nurse Morris… gave up feeling balls and giving kids the six needles, and went to work in an ammunition company making missiles and bullets and bombs to rid the world of the human race.

Big Murphy and his gang… started a boy band and reached number 5 in the UK charts with their self-penned hit: *'Hit Me With Your Baseball Bat All Night Long'*. And the B side: *'Giz Me Your Dinner Money Butt, So I Can Go And Buy Some Blackjacks'*.

Dekka's mam and dad… still enjoy a bowl of Smash, still argue about Alan the Midget, and they still live in the 70's.

Dekka's brother… is still an IT executive working in Milton Keynes and apparently, he's still a twat!!!

Doctor Quirk... is still a real doctor.

Thank you and all that jazz!!!

Firstly, I must say a massive 'thank you' to **Laura Mochan** who actually 'volunteered' to sort out my crap spelling and grammar. She said, *'No wonder you always had F- when writing stories.'*

A huge shout out to **The Off-It Reality** for illustrating the front cover....a real talented man behind the mask. And another thank you a million to **Marc Phillips** for designing another great cover....luvs you man xx

Also, I would like to acknowledge the input from **Neil Maidman** and the cast from **Gurnwah Productions** who helped colour in some of these fables and personalities when we were rehearsing it for the stage play version of the book.

I would like to thank all my old schoolteachers, (the good, the bad and the insane), the nuns (invisible shiver running up my spine) and my old school mates who went to Bishop Hedley High School who consciously, or unconsciously, made this story come to life.

Stay Free

Bunko x

Other titles by Anthony Bunko

- The Tale of the Shagging Monkeys – Trippin'

- Two Shagging Monkeys – The Siege of El Rancho

- The Belt of Kings

- Boy, Girl, Fruitcake, Flower (renamed – TV, Tarot Cards and George bloody Clooney)

- Working up to the Slaughterhouse

- *Demons and Cocktails - Stuart Cable's autobiography*

- *Hugh Laurie Biography*

- *Hugh Jackman Biography*

- *2 Hard to Handle – the autobiography of Mike Spikey Watkins*

- *Deadwalker*

- Dic Penderyn and the Merthyr Rising.

- Lord Forgive me but I was a Bullshit Consultant

- *Ma'am Anna – Anna Rodriguez's autobiography*

- *Nerves of Steele – the Story of Phil Steele*

- The Boy who Cried Sheep

- The Wizard of GurnOZ

- Frayed Around The Edges

Printed in Poland
by Amazon Fulfillment
Poland Sp. z o.o., Wrocław